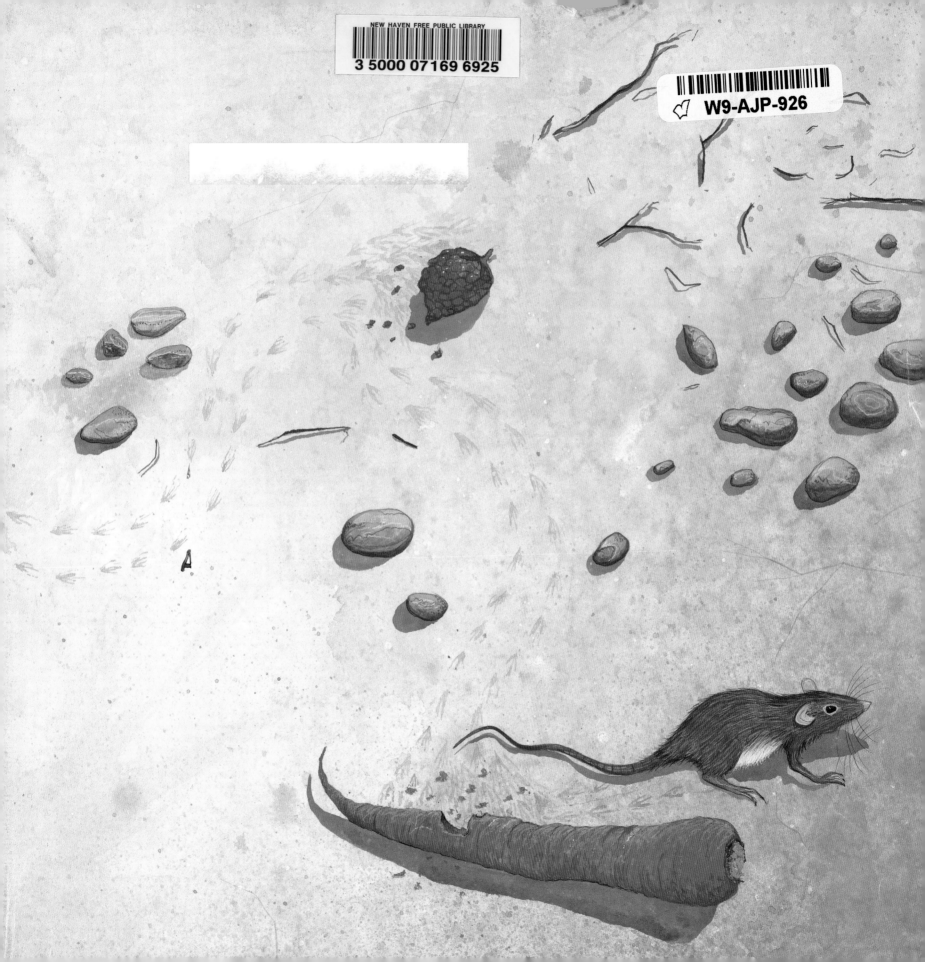

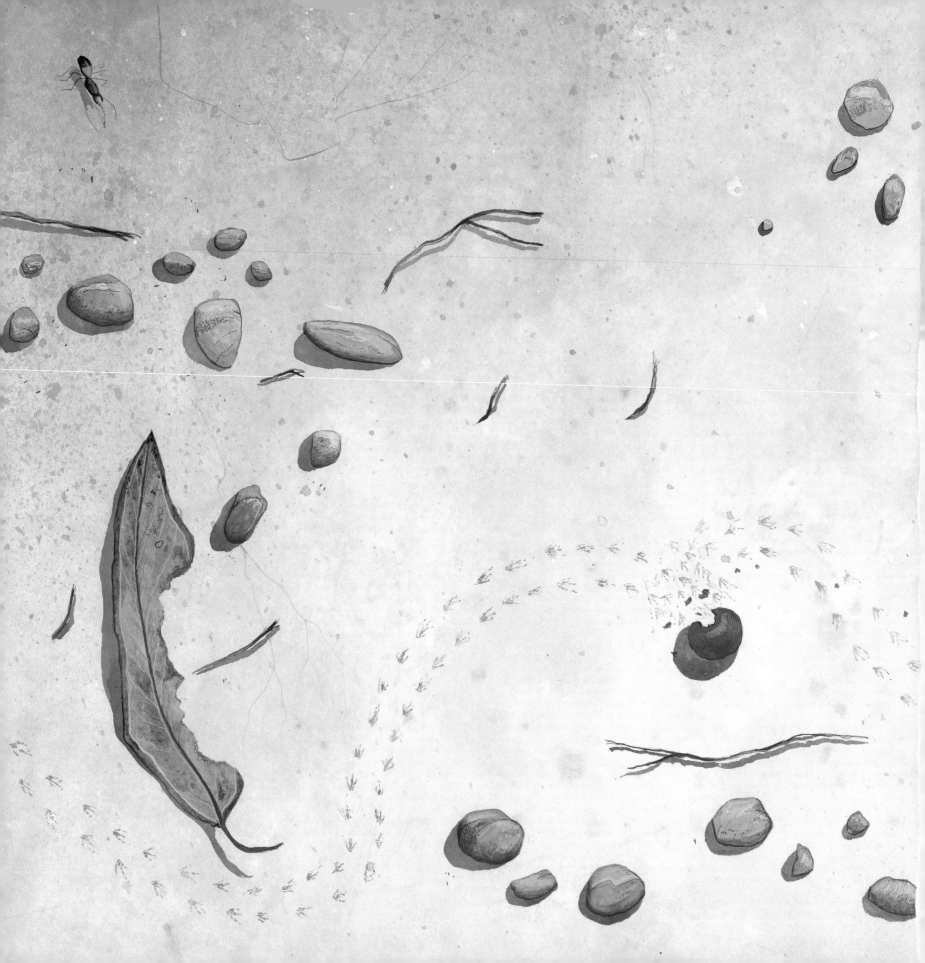

The Old Woman
Who Loved to Read

John Winch

Holiday House/New York

In a small farmhouse in the country lived an old woman who loved to read.

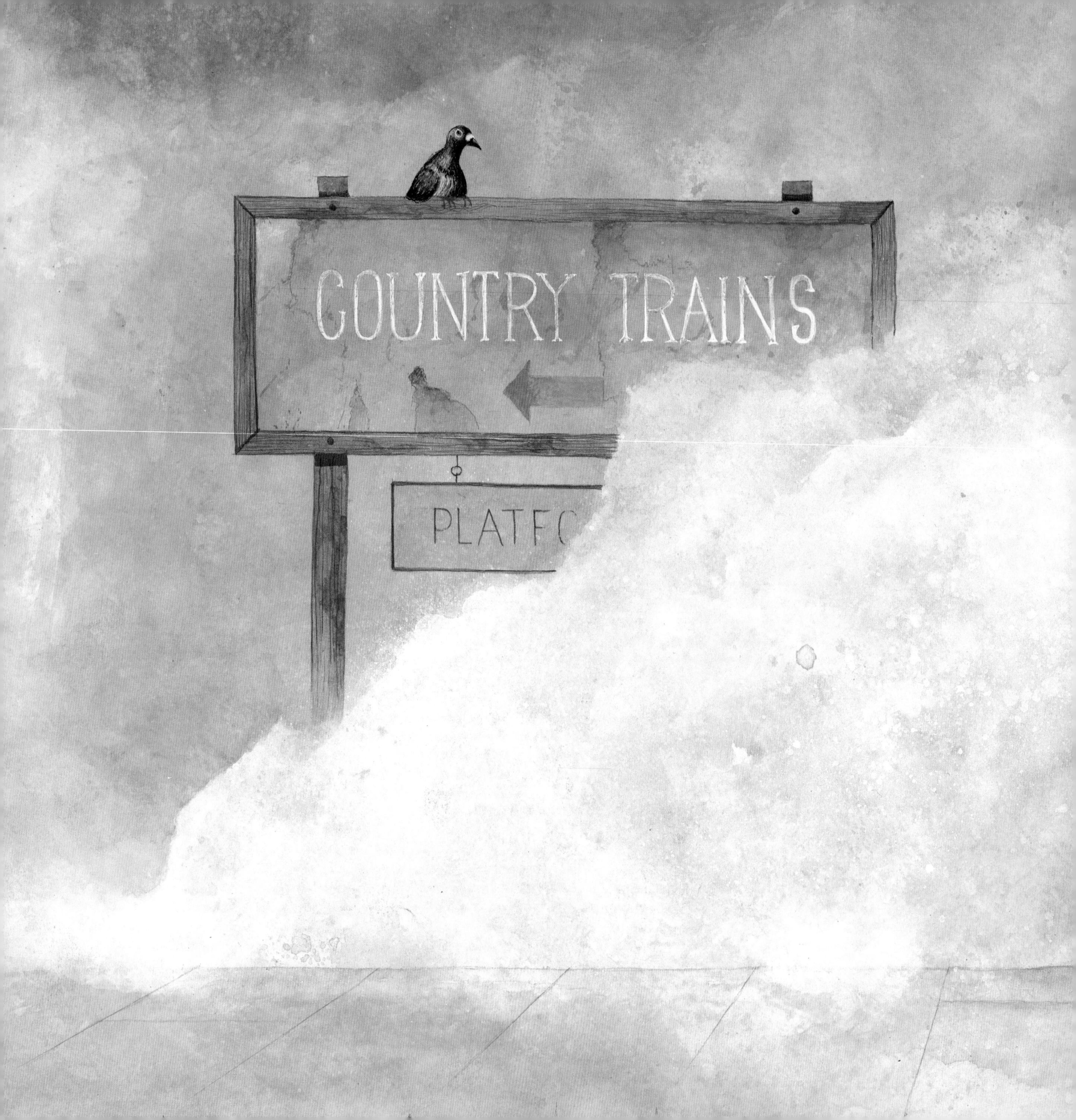
COUNTRY TRAINS
PLATFO

She had once lived in the city, but life there was no longer quiet and peaceful, so she decided to move.

In her new home she had many chores, both inside . . .

and out.

In spring she had an unexpected visitor

who was very demanding

and stayed on until summer.

In summer the old woman thought she would have time at last to read, but the fruit needed harvesting

and had to be preserved for the coming seasons.

The summer was hot and very, very dry.

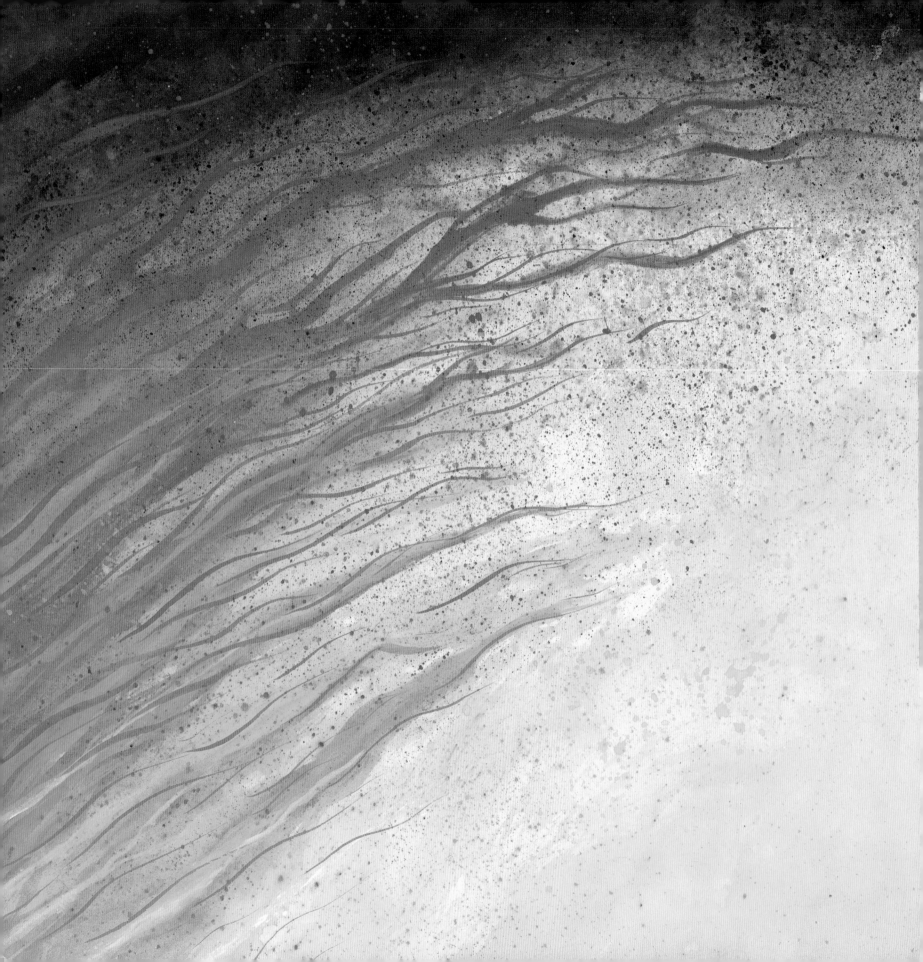

She had intended to read in the autumn but the rains came early

and lasted throughout the winter.

But in the heart of winter when she had finished all her tasks, tended the animals and stocked the larder, all was quiet and peaceful

and the old woman
could enjoy her reading.

Books to Read
The Wind in the Willows ✓
The Secret Garden
Gulliver's Travels ✓
The Pied Piper
Come by Chance
A Winter's Tale
Humphrey Clinker
Oliver Twist
Seven Little Aust...ans
Eleanor Eliz...

First published by Scholastic Australia Pty Limited in 1996. This edition published
under license from Scholastic Australia Pty Limited.

First published in the United States by Holiday House in 1997.

Printed and bound in Hong Kong

Library of Congress Cataloging-in-Publication Data
Winch, John, 1944–
   The old woman who loved to read/John Winch.
      p.   cm.
   Summary: An old woman moves to the country in order to have a
peaceful life with lots of time to read but soon finds that each
season brings other tasks to keep her busy.
   ISBN 0-8234-1281-4 (hardcover: alk. paper)
   [1. Old age — Fiction.   2. Animals — Fiction.   3. Country life —
Australia — Fiction.   4. Australia — Fiction.]   I. Title.
PZ7.W72185Ok   1997   96-19665   CIP   AC
[E] — dc20

6925

MAY 1 9 1998